MW00487993

The
Silence
is
the
Noise

The
Silence
is
the
Noise

by Bart Schaneman

Trident Press
Boulder, CO

Published by Trident Press
940 Pearl St.
Boulder, CO 80302

ISBN: 978-0-9992499-6-3

Cover art by Marsha Robinson (IG: @strangedirt)
Layout by Nathaniel Kennon Perkins

For Nammin

Before the job. Before Lucy. Before any of it — I tell myself I'm not going to stay. I'm returning to my hometown to live cheaply while I wait to hear back from literary agents about my novel. Once that's published I'm headed back to the coast.

The van from the airport crests the ridgeline of the pine tree hills, and I can see Winterborn spread out on the valley floor below. It looks so little. The sight excited me once. Everything I knew was there — the low buildings, the river winding through the two towns, the monument off to the side — but now it only seems small, limited and limiting. I don't know if this is a good decision.

The van drops me at a pay-by-the-week motel, a relic from the '50s where you can drive your car right to the door. It was nice at one point, but not anymore. I check in, toss my backpack on the bed, and take a breath. Aside from a diesel truck that rattles the walls when it passes and a lowrider with a trunk full of subwoofers that rolls by, the whistle of wind gusts in the windows is the only outside noise. It's easier to breathe and stifling at the same time.

I need to buy a car, so I leave the motel and head south, walking through the neighborhoods, aware that if anyone I know sees me walking they'll likely think it strange. Probably figure I had car trouble. People don't walk in this town unless they're retired and can afford to waste time, or can't afford to scrape together the money for a car. There's not much at all for public transportation, so I don't have a choice.

My walking route takes me through a neighborhood of well-off families. Large, ranch-style homes, most of them brick, with tall privacy fences and perfectly mowed lawns. The past is an ocean, coming in waves, unbidden. From the sea floor rises the church from my childhood. The place of my confirmation, of weddings and funerals and Sunday services. Then the next block a house where a friend from school lived, swimming with more memories, watery shapes swaying in the current.

I cross over into the part of town where most of the poor folk live. Pass houses with short chain-link fences, dogs chained to porches, and patchy lawns for a half dozen blocks until I come up on a lot of newly washed cars, trucks and SUVs. I spot an old orange Chevy Silverado with less than 200,000 miles for $3,000. A little rust on the fenders but it'll do.

After two weeks in the motel I find a house that sits up on the edge of the valley. An old split-level with a deck in disrepair. From the deck I can peer out over the two towns split by the river with the hills and the large bluff on the far side. Across the valley to the horizon snow still clings to the pine trees, and geese fly in thin Vs then circle and glide to land among the cornfields and ponds by the river. I watch the cars and trucks pass through town on the highway. Above all of it white streaks of jet contrails spread out over the valley and expand into feathery bands of fluorescent color as the sun sets.

I start work tomorrow and I'm pendulum-swinging back and forth from anticipation to dread. I'm eager to learn, but anxious about confronting who I used to be when I grew up in this town. We all have moments in life we're ashamed of, and mine aren't any better or worse than anyone else's, but a lot of us leave home and don't come back, so we're not living with the chance that our history will walk up to us and spit in our face, remind us of who we were. But I'm willing to endure it if it means getting what I'm after.

My whole goal, my dream, my desired purpose in life is to become a novelist. It's all I want. And I'm willing to do pretty much anything to help me achieve that goal. Journalism. Moving back to my hometown. Whatever path I need to take to get to a life of writing books I'm willing to do it. I'll sacrifice anything. That's what really brings me back to Winterborn. But I'm probably not going to tell very many people that.

I want to become a regional writer in a

way that's not reductive, but means that I understand one place, one region well enough to write about the plants, the animals, the sky, the weather, and, most importantly, the people in it. What drives them. I want to do for my part of the world what other writers have done for theirs. My plan is to work as a reporter, talk to the people where I'm from, learn about their lives, and use the material for my first book.

A year and a half ago I started a novel in California, trying to employ the technique of leaving a place to learn how to write about it. But my material was thin. I needed to understand this place better. I want to know more. I want to live here and gather more material about the place that I'm from and use it to finish this book. Once it's published I'll keep traveling the region and continue to write about Winterborn from afar until I have built an entire place of characters of my creation.

I want as much as anything to write a good book, one that will sell enough to allow me to move back to the coast and be close to the ocean again. I think that if I can be a good enough writer and get a book deal I can live wherever I choose. It's writing as salvation. My way to get the life of freedom I seek. Because I want more than anything to get free. To live on my own terms.

And so, tomorrow I start at the newspaper and write about the people here so I can learn about them. Live among my old friends from high school who stayed, or who left and came back, like me. Communicating the whole time through email with agents in New York who write me saying "we certainly don't get a lot of novels set in this region. This is interesting, but we need you to work on your storyline. And this character. It needs to be more convincing."

During the day I'll work to learn how to become a reporter, and at night I'll work on the novel. Seems pretty simple, right?

Right when I moved here I emailed a story to the editor of the town's daily newspaper on spec. The pitch was an essay about coming home, with a few positive observations, but mostly it contained correctives, prescriptions, challenges to the culture. I talked about how I had grown up on a farm and how that had benefited my life in ways I never could have expected, but that the town needed to adapt or it would die.

The editor's response was curt:

I'm interested. Not sure we can run this, but send me a resume and give me a few days to come up with an assignment. — Guy

A day later I walked downtown toward the town's only bookstore. My phone buzzed. The email came in direct.

Subject: Assignment

> *Here's what I want you to do. Judging by your background, you seem to have an interest in culture, literature, music, and all that. Not important right now. What I want you to do is focus on the people in the community. Profile. Find out who people are. Why they live here. What they think about the community. But positive people. Success stories. We don't want people in the paper who are going to run down our way of life.*

> *Assignment: A story on five people who have returned to Scottsbluff to live, work. Only people raised here. 250 words on each. With your local connections I'm sure you can make it work. Deadline one*

week from today. Take pictures if you can.
   Best luck,
   Guy

Already I have my apprehensions about this job. Do I want to become a journalist? Maybe, but I don't want to work in offices my whole life. And I'm unsure I can approach people and ask them hard questions about their lives. At least the first assignment is to talk to my old friends. That's pretty easy.

So I call up a friend who's a teacher, another who's taken a job as an associate in her father's law firm, and one who works for the railroad.

Then I go on Facebook and do a search for all my remaining mutual friends who live in town. I send them messages explaining the project. A couple of those politely refuse, citing the typical Midwestern reasoning that they don't feel comfortable talking about themselves and "besides my life really isn't that interesting."

But I do get a few positive responses, friends of friends, or classmates that don't dislike me from high school. By that I mean

I had a hard time in high school and it came out in a lot of different, unfortunate ways. Hostility, mostly. I wasn't always the nicest guy to be around.

So I go to their places of work, or to their homes, where nearly all of them say they came back because this is a good place to raise kids, that they enjoy being close to family, and the low cost of living means that they have more time to enjoy their lives. They find living here easy, no one sits in traffic to get anywhere, they enjoy playing a role in the community, and when they want to they can easily drive to Colorado or South Dakota for a good time. The majority of people I interview have golden tickets to successful careers. Some of them want exactly what they're getting. Others have compromised to raise families or take what they think is the path of least resistance.

After publishing the story, Guy offers me a staff job. Starting pay of $22,500 a year. Never going to last, but it will at least pay my rent in Winterborn. Over the phone, before I start, Guy suggests I write about the places I know from my childhood. He says he can tell

I'm a "literary guy who can write" but that he'll have to teach me how to report. I say I'm in.

So it's my first day of work. The Sun-Gazette building is at the end of the row of short buildings on Main Street. To the south runs the river and between the river and my new office the railroad. Across the street sits a long boarded-up train station. It's been decades since a commuter train stopped here. Now trains with black cars full of coal chug back and forth from Wyoming.

Inside the newsroom, desks are dispersed in no discernible pattern, loosely grouped by department. The hourly workers toil out on the floor where they're exposed to all manner of behavior from their coworkers. Men curse at uncooperative computers. Salesmen make obnoxiously friendly sales calls. Reporters stare at blinking cursors, sigh, pound the desk trying to come up with brilliant ledes while blocking out the noise. Around the perimeter the managers' offices are protected by the most sought-after of all job perks: doors.

My small desk sits in the middle of a row of three journalists. To my right Jerry, the assistant editor. To the left Carl, for decades the staff photographer, now, he tells me, forced to write stories along with taking pictures. I quietly take out my notebook, place it by my phone, and log in.

Momentary pockets of sound erupt all around me.

A customer enters upset that her paper hasn't been delivered. "This is the third time in two weeks!" she yells at the secretary. "I don't even know why I pay for your rag anymore. If it wasn't for the obituaries your paper would be useless!"

Jerry says to himself "you need to check those every morning just so you know you're not dead!"

He begins to sing to the tune of "Hello Muddah, Hello Faddah":

I hate people

They all suck
They act like I give a fuck...

Across the room a graphic designer argues with an ad rep in the creative department. "If you don't give me a ticket, then how am I supposed to know that I need to build your ad?" the designer says.

"The ticket is right there under that giant bag of fast food shit you're eating," the ad rep retorts. "Maybe if you cared as much about designing ads as you do about quarter pounders we wouldn't have this problem."

"Maybe," the designers says under her breath as he walks away, "go take a flying leap at a rolling donut."

Jerry unrolls a sheet of bubble wrap from under his desk and absentmindedly pops the plastic blisters. His phone voice carries from the breakroom to the front door. "Well, can you please tell the good sheriff to give me a call back whenever he's done getting cats down from trees or pulling people over on the speed trap up by the hospital or whatever it is he does all day?" He turns to me and says "Law enforcement in this town thinks they can get away with whatever they want! Well, they can't!" POP! POP! POP!

I nod and return to searching the internet for contacts to add to my Rolodex. As the day rolls on the building clears out. Sales reps make client visits, reporters meet sources for interviews, managers golf or sneak home to watch TV and take naps. I do the bulk of my writing in the late afternoon, when it's the quietest. I file a preview on a magician at the community theater a few minutes before deadline.

Headed out to the canal with a six pack in my backseat I see Lucy Schmidt driving a purple Toyota Tacoma. I want to wave but don't. We're friends on Facebook, have been for years, but when I take out my phone to message her, writing "hey, saw you driving around town, want to meet for coffee?" I don't send it. Surely she knows I've come back. People in Winterborn still read the newspaper.

I park my truck on the canal road and sit on the box. Across the valley the bluff is backlit in yellow. This region, a long time ago given the name the Great American Desert, was once the grazing land for thousands, if not millions of American bison. Buffalo. Native American tribes lived off of the herds. Evidence of them running great numbers of stampeding buffalo through canyons and over cliffs is still buried under the prairie grass north of town. The bones of a species that belonged here well before we learned how to pump water. The pioneers came through this land pulling wagons, sick, starving, filthy, desperate, looking for the landmark the Lakota Sioux called Elk Penis. It looked more like a chimney before the Civil War-era soldiers used it for cannon practice, or so the story goes.

Then came the Germans from Russia. Half of my ancestors. The men and women of a people once from Bavaria who came to the Volga River valley as farmers, who were then persecuted when the deal was no longer honored. So, as refugees, they fled to America with the goal of seeking out a land, a climate favorable to their style of farming. They found something close — sandy soil, little rain — but the land was cheap. An irrigation system was developing and sugar beets were profitable. So they married others like them, had a dozen children to help work the fields and those children married other Volga Germans. They sang German in church, passed down recipes for the old foods — cabbage burgers and grebel and dinna kuchen — and took to building a life in America where they could be anybody. Bloodlines started over. Family names meant little — they had been changed on the way over anyway — and the past, life in Russia particularly, didn't warrant much conversation. Everyone looked to the future, to the constant opportunity and promise of the new world. Who knew what the people were who followed the Queen to Russia. Failures? Those desperate enough to change their circumstances that dramatically? Or were they pioneers? Bold, enterprising. Who cared? All that mattered in those early days in Winterborn was work and money and food and land.

My phone vibrates in my jeans pocket.

"Ethan Thomas!" Carrick Williams says. "I heard you came back. Why'd you do that?"

"Hard to say."

"You dumbass."

"So you're happy I'm home then."

"Hell yes I'm happy you're home. Just hope you know what you're getting into. Anyway, we can get deep later. I'm having people over to my place tomorrow night. You should come."

"Who's going to be there?"

"A few people. You'll know some of them. Just come. You know where I live."

"Hello? Yes. Hello. Hi. This is Mary Winslow. I need to speak to a reporter."

"I'm a reporter, ma'am. How can I help you?"

"I live at 7984 Spring Creek Road in Arikaree, and I've been watching huge tanker trucks pass my house. Fracker trucks. I live on the north side of town and they've been tearing up and down the highway for weeks. More of 'em everyday."

"Do you happen to know what they're hauling, ma'am? It's not oil, is it?"

"Fracking water, I'm pretty sure."

"Fracking water?"

"Yes. The water they get when they're done fracking. I'm not an expert. I'm sure you can talk to someone who knows more than me. Come up here and take a look for yourself. People oughta know what's happening here."

"Will do. Thanks for the phone call, Miss Winslow."

I check over my notes then gather my camera bag. At the whiteboard I move the marker from In to Out and write "gone to Arikaree to check on 'frackers.'"

I back my truck in at the mouth of a driveway, turn off the engine. A Cooper's hawk perches on a powerline up the road, scanning the pastureland for voles. Whatever else it can kill. All patience. Singularity of purpose. Thin, stringy clouds spread across the metal blue sky.

The radio host gives the markets then segues to a song about sitting on a tailgate, waiting for the fish to bite. I turn it down. Take out my notebook to order my thoughts. I've just paraphrased an Emerson quote when a truck blows past, the wind from it enough to push my window in a little. I follow it.

I catch it at the next mile marker and take out my phone, activate the voice recorder app.

"Six-wheel truck. Tanker. Colorado plates. Triangle placard that reads "Hazardous Waste." North of Arikaree about five miles..."

A rock kicks up from the back tire and skitters and bounces, on a direct line for my windshield. It hits the bug guard. Up and over. I back off.

After a few miles the trucker puts on the blinker, turns into an unmarked driveway. He punches in a code to open the chainlink gate. I snap a few photos through the windshield then gun it, following the tanker in. The gate swings closed just as I slide through.

The road into the pasture dips then rises to a plateau where large square bales form a perimeter around an old oil well. Three rust-colored water tanks stand sentry around the center. The truck I'm following halts at the mouth of the bales. The driver steps out, walks to the back of his rig, clearly waiting for me to pull closer.

When I do, the man approaches. He wears a mustache that horseshoes down to his jawline. Spits as I power down my window.

"You lost, son?"

"Actually, no. I'm a reporter for the Sun-Gazette and I was hoping to find out a little bit about what you guys are doing here."

"So you are lost then."

"What's in the truck?"

"I ain't talking to you. I suggest you turn around."

"Can you at least tell me what company you work for?"

"It says on my hat." Raptor Oil. "Now you better get and get off this property before you find yourself in some kind of trouble."

"Do you have anyone I can call with the company?"

"Google it. I'm sure your type can figure it out."

"Do you know who owns this land?"

"We're done here, pal. Best get moving."

The trucker steps away, points back the way we came in.

Back at the office, I set my bag down and say to no one in particular "there's something weird happening north of Arikaree."

"Like what? Aliens again?" Jerry asks. "Last time they thought it was aliens it was just people flying remote control airplanes at night."

"Like weird stuff. Not sure it's legal."

"Maybe you can be a bit more vague."

"A bunch of trucks with hazardous waste placards and Colorado plates hauling something onto or off of a random pasture up there."

"Really? Who told you that?"

"I saw it myself. Followed them to the site. Got turned away."

Jerry stands up and walks into Guy's office. I hear them talking as I click my memory card into the reader.

"The new kid might have just lucked onto a big story. I don't think he's ready to write it. Might need some help."

"Get out of here, Jerry," Guy says. "You probably would have caught this one yourself if you ever answered the phone."

"If he screws it up don't say I didn't warn you."

Jerry saunters over to my desk.

"The bossman thinks you can handle this. I'm not sure. But I'm going to be really busy shooting sports this week or else I'd help. I also don't really do co-bylines. I'm sure you won't screw it up. Or maybe you will. What's your lede going to be?"

"I don't know yet. I still need to finish my reporting."

"Maybe you don't have a story then."

I thought about how to respond.

"Looks like you just had a brain fart."

"Just thinking."

"Right."

I Google "Raptor oil," then spend part of the afternoon searching through websites and news articles.

I learn:

Raptor is a major hydraulic fracturing company based in Denver, according to the company's website.

- It has multiple drilling operations in Colorado and Oklahoma.
- One of its operations was shut down in Weld County, Colorado. The wastewater the company injected back into the ground after fracking

the process "lubricated" a faultline and caused a small earthquake, the Coloradoan newspaper reported.

- The company had been sued by a homeowners' association in Thornton, Colorado, after it was found that a leak in a wastewater injection well contaminated the ground around a number of new homes, according to a story in the Denver Post.

What do I know about fracking? I watched a documentary once set in Pennsylvania where the people who lived there could light their tap water on fire after the frackers had released natural gas into the well system. But this would be a first for western Nebraska. Oil prices aren't up enough for it to be profitable to drill. So what is it? I decide to take what I have to Guy.

"Sounds like a mess," he says over his shoulder, facing the wall on his little computer, putting the finishing touches on his editorial on deadline, a time of the day I haven't yet learned to avoid. "Call the county. Find out if any permits have been filed. Then call the oil and gas commission and find out what they say."

The deputy director at the oil and gas commission office tells me that yes, a company from Colorado has a permit to dump wastewater from hydraulic fracturing oil extraction. The water is injected about a mile in the ground, in the layers of old seabed from millions of years ago, when the area had been an inland sea. The commissioner assures me it's all perfectly safe. He offers to fax the permit so I don't have to call the county for it.

Guy looks at the information and says, "You don't have to write it tonight unless you think you're going to get scooped."

"I doubt it. Unless Jerry steals it from me."

"He's too lazy for that. You need another source, though. Call the university and talk to a scientist."

In the morning I speak with a geologist who once worked as a petroleum engineer. He assures me the project is perfectly safe.

I try to figure out how to write this. The geologist obviously loves oil. The commissioners' jobs are dependent on oil and gas activity. I can't make up what I want them to say, but I kind of feel like they're full of shit. The best way to balance it is to include Raptor's company history. Its screw ups and issues. So people know what could happen. In its environmental impact statement, Raptor said it could be hauling thousands of gallons of highly salinated water a day, with up to 80 trucks coming in and out when the operation is at full capacity. I use quotes from my interviews and weave in details of the application.

For a comment, I call the rancher whose name is listed on the permit.

"Is Dale Falconer there?"

"This is he."

"Hi Dale. This is Ethan Thomas. I'm a reporter for the Sun-Gazette."

"Hi Ethan. How are your parents doing? I went to school with your dad."

"They're good. Thanks. Loving Arizona about now."

"I'll bet."

"Reason I'm calling, I'm working on a story about the wastewater injection on your land."

Silence.

"Are you still there? I was wondering if you could comment?"

"I'm not sure that's anyone's business."

"I'm sorry, sir, but we've had people calling in asking about what those trucks are hauling."

"I wish you wouldn't put that in the paper."

"It could be important if the trucks are damaging the roads and the water has an impact on the environment," I say, wishing immediately I hadn't phrased it that way. I know he'll bristle at that. "People seem concerned."

"Is that what you're writing?"

"I'm just relaying some of the concerns I've heard."

"So what are you writing?"

"Is that an abandoned oil well you're using?"

"I really don't see how this is anyone's business."

"Can you at least confirm that?"

"Yes. I hope you're not causing me a bunch of trouble, Ethan."

"Just doing my job."

"You don't have anything else you could write about? How about you write about how the school district is paying for its unnecessary new school on the backs of farmers and ranchers?"

"Like I said, sir, this seems to be of interest to our readers."

"Please don't quote me in anything you write."

"No sir. Thanks for your time. I appreciate it."

The line goes dead.

I write up what I have and move it over on the system, then stop in Guy's office to tell him the story's in. He grunts in affirmation.

The following morning I check my story. Guy has edited it, rewritten the lede and crafted a better headline but changed little else. I feel this story has potential. "Legs," I think journalists say.

"Your story could have used some more digging," Jerry says in passing. "But not bad."

An hour later the news clerk processes an item for the community calendar that reads:

Wastewater injection meeting

Keeler's shed. Two miles north of Arikaree.
Saturday. Noon. Pulled pork sandwiches.
It's my Saturday to work so I make plans
to go.

Carrick's house is a two-story, split level with front and back yards and an attached two-car garage. I don't know anybody my age living in cities who could afford to own an entire house. But in Winterborn my friends all have nice homes with large yards and garages. Not sure yet if the trade off is worth it. I ring the bell then walk in.

"What's up, man?" Carrick says, hugging me.

Carrick's dark hair is short now, and he keeps a trimmed beard. He looks like he's been lifting — his shoulders and chest filled out. He also looks like he's been drinking plenty. The bags under his eyes almost black.

I follow him into the kitchen, where he cuts up limes for Pacificos.

"Do I know anyone here?" I ask.

"I'm sure you'll recognize a few people." He hands me a beer. I follow him into the living room where a few guys I used to know watch a televised baseball game on mute. Country music plays low on the stereo. The subject of conversation is town sports.

"That Johnson kid's already hanging on the rim," Lane says from the couch. "In seventh grade."

"He's a beast," Rusty says. "Just like his older brother. He'll be all-state if he stays off the grass."

"His brother made it," Carrick says. "And I'm pretty sure he was stoned for half the games."

"I heard the high school team has a chance of making state this year," I say.

The guys laugh.

"Ethan Thomas," Lane says, "Just got back in town and already an expert on all things Winterborn."

"Hey I'm just telling you what I heard from the sports guys at the paper."

"Right. Like anyone at the Sun-Gazette knows what the hell's going on," Rusty says.

"The Huskers have a better chance of winning the national championship than the Wildcats making it to state."

"So you're a reporter there now?" Lane asks.

"Just started."

"I heard they don't pay very well."

"That's correct. The pay's pretty shitty. It's not a long-term thing. I'm just trying to learn how to write."

"You want to be a writer?" Lane asks.

"A novelist," I say.

"You don't know shit about writing," Rusty says.

"Ethan 'Shakespeare' Thomas," Lane says. "From the farm to the best-seller list."

"Ethan 'Woodward and Bernstein' Thomas," Rusty says. "Can't wait until the Sun-Gazette wins its first Pulitzer."

"Can't wait until they figure out how to spell," Lane says. "And go more than one day without a correction."

"But hey," Rusty says, "The paper makes a great firestarter."

"And bird-cage liner."

"And window cleaner."

"Maybe you guys should try actually reading something once in your lives," Carrick says.

"I read a book once," Rusty says. "That was enough of that. TV's better."

This night is a perfect example of why I wasn't sure if I should come back in the first place. High school belonged to the guys who were good at sports, and these guys still carried themselves as though that mattered. My teenage years were not nearly as easy. I came to high school from the country, elementary and junior high school spent out in school among the corn and bean fields. The next four years were a constant test, one that I only finished but didn't answer every question correctly. Before I came back I wasn't sure I wanted to be reminded of all that struggle, no matter how subtle.

I resolve on the way home that the way to overcome that and correct the mistakes in my past will be to publicly succeed at this job. To have the whole community read me every day. To become a good reporter and show all my peers what I truly am, and always was, capable of.

The wind whines in my truck windows as I drive home. No cars on the streets. The lights off in the houses, only the street lamps and the stars and the gusts to guide me home.

I park near the driveway of the lot. Last in, first out. People mostly drive dust-coated full-sized trucks. The door to the quonset is slid open enough for a person to get in. I stand on the edge of the crowd with my notebook. People sit on folding chairs at the two rows of banquet tables. Along the wall a table holds a slow cooker with pulled pork, a platter of white bread hamburger buns, squeeze bottles of barbecue sauce, individual bags of potato chips and a cooler of canned pop and water.

After most of the people have their food a middle-aged man in jeans and a plaid shirt stands in front of the pork and calls the room to attention.

"Hey now," he says. "I want to thank everybody for coming by. We have Dale Falconer here, who owns the land where you've seen the trucks and the water tanks. He's agreed to tell us what's going on and answer your questions."

Dale stands next to the farmer. He's dressed similarly but is shorter and more round.

"Now I just want to say that before we begin no one here is fracking," Falconer says. "Hell I don't even know if you can frack this land. I used to drill for oil on my property but the well failed must've been twenty years back. I was approached about a year ago by this outfit down in Colorado who said they wanted to repurpose my old well to inject saltwater into the ground. That's what they get when they frack, a bunch of excess water, and they dispose of it by putting it back in the earth. We went over the science behind it and they assured me there's nothing to worry about."

"So what exactly are the trucks hauling?" asks a large man in overalls.

"And where's it going?" lobs a curly-haired woman wearing a Sturgis motorcycle rally t-shirt.

"Wastewater. Into the ground. About a mile down," Falconer says.

"Through the aquifer?" comes a voice Ethan can't place.

"The pipe is triple-cased in concrete through the aquifer then shoots about another 5,000 feet past it to an open geologic layer, they tell me."

"So what are we supposed to do about what these trucks are doing to the roads?" overalls asks.

"Jim, you're not supposed to do anything about it. I pay taxes to use these roads same as you."

"And what do you do if one these trucks spills?"

"They have insurance."

The crowd doesn't seem to have any more immediate questions.

"I want to thank you all for coming out," Falconer says. "I know you have valid concerns. But I wouldn't have done this if I thought it was going to hurt me or anyone else."

"How much are you making on the deal?"

the curly-haired woman sneaks in.

"I think we're done here," Falconer says. "I hope you enjoyed the sandwiches. Meat came from my hogs."

I walk around and take down the names, ages and occupations of the people who asked questions. I get a picture of Falconer talking to a semi-circle of folks with their arms folded. Then I gather comments from a couple more people as they finish their lunch.

The general sentiment is "We'll have to look into this more but if it's negatively impacting anything just so one guy gets rich then we don't like it."

Falconer heads for the door. When I catch him he only says "who invited you? Are you going to make me need a lawyer? I said what I wanted to say. No further comment." He gets in his truck and leaves.

On the drive back to the office I have a good 15 minutes to think. The sky is empty, open, clean, not enough to catch my interest. So I think down, to underneath the truck, past the wheels and asphalt through the first layers of sediment and rock, a few hundred feet down, to the waters of the aquifer, the vast underground ocean of freshwater that expands north, east and south from the western edge of Nebraska.

What does this water source mean to this country, to these people? The most iconic of their prairie symbols, the windmill, was created to draw water up from this underground ocean to fill circular metal tanks and quench the thirst of the blank angus and charolais and hereford cattle of the land. Sprinklers spin in concentric crop circles misting corn and beans and sugar beets with the fossil energy from the earth. I dive deeper until I reach the ground at the bottom of the aquifer. I hike through a maze of canyons under an endless sky. I summit a mountain and nearly hit my head on the rock ceiling. I become aware of how water is energy, how this underground ocean is nonrenewable, a dinosaur of life that could make this land, this place once known as the Great American Desert, bloom and feed millions. We conquered this arid land with this water, and now someone wants to risk it.

At the office, a sports editor sits at his desk under a dim light listening to a game on the radio. I sit and select three photos to attach to the story. Then I start a blank document. I begin with my byline - By Ethan Thomas, a practice I compare to the chef's trick of cutting up an onion to begin cooking without a recipe or meal in mind, to get the creative energy flowing.

If I can just get a first sentence started I can write. But aside from the byline I don't see a clear path forward. Until I contemplate the people at the gathering and their quotes and what Falconer said. I'm green, but I have already learned from Guy not to start the story with the fact that a crowd gathered. "What's the news?" I can hear Guy asking. "What's the point?" The news is that Falconer has revealed what the trucks are doing. I start there then work in the concerns of the community members.

Once I begin to write I gain steady momentum, consulting my notebook for color and quotes, extremely focused, brimming with pleasure and purpose, completely unaware of the time that's passing until, after I include all of the relevant detail and utterings from my notes, as well as the background research I have on Raptor, their fires and explosions and moratoriums for causing earthquakes, I have a 25-inch story that I'm hoping will be well-read. I print it and walk outside to the picnic table to read it over, pumping my leg as I read, thinking about nothing but whether I got everything right and if I can improve what I've already written.

I clean up the typos and shorten a few sentences then send it over to Guy. While I wait, I log the obituaries and process them for Sunday's paper, making style corrections and sending over revisions to the funeral homes.

Guy's email comes back about 30 minutes later with a revised version attached.

"Needed some tightening," he writes. "And you spelled public without an 'l'. That's one you don't want to do again. Tell the desk to put it on Page 1."

I swap my story in the system with Guy's edited version. It shrinks from 25 inches to 17. Disappointing but I can't argue with Guy's edits. He's improved it. I grab a marker and write Wastewater Meeting with a red P1 ↑ on the whiteboard. I shoulder my camera bag and walk out to the parking lot, energized, ready for more.

At the Civic Center, I'm wearing the gray Oxford shirt from the day I graduated from college. After the bride and groom's dance I notice Lucy out in the hallway. The navy blue dress she wears looks slightly faded, just like my shirt. I offer to buy her a drink.

"What are you doing home?" I ask.

"Jesus. Not you, too," she says, giving me a quick hug.

"You're tan," I say.

"Just spent three months in Hawaii. But so are you."

"I did a little traveling before I came home."

"Then you know my pain. How ugly is it here?"

"Is it?"

"Compared to the ocean? Are you kidding?"

"No, you're right. I'm just happy to be talking to someone my own age."

We carry drinks to a table. Before we sit down she says, "dance with me." She grabs my hand and leads me to the dance floor. I can see the bride through the crowd, with her shoes off in her white gown, two-stepping, flushed and happy.

"So is this what it would be like to be in a relationship here?" I ask. "Come to weddings. Dance on Saturday nights. Church on Sunday."

"Oh no," she says. "Much worse. Mostly television and sports. Themed coed baby showers."

"That's pretty dark."

"You're going to regret coming back."

"I think I already do."

We dance a little more. I finish my drink. Then Lucy's parents are ready to go home and she offers to go with them.

"Just like high school," she says. "Call me tomorrow. We'll go do something."

Late the next morning, I'm bored of sending out query letters to literary agents so I call. Lucy picks up the phone laughing. It's almost rude. She sounds like she's protecting herself.

"You really should get your own phone,"

I say.

"Cell phones give you brain cancer. The radiation seeps into your skull. But hi," she says.

"I can come pick you up this afternoon."

"Can you come pick me up now? I need to get out of here."

I'm not sure why I give into that demand but I do. I clean out my truck as best I can. Throw away receipts and empty cups and wipe off the dash. Then I drive over the dirt roads with my windows down, looking out over the land. In a place like this you notice the sky as much as anything. I pull up to her house and a Lab runs up and circles my truck. The dog sniffs me as I walk up to the door. I love dogs and this one reminds me of my childhood. Lucy comes out before I can knock.

"I know a place," I say.

I take her over to the creek a mile from the farm my parents used to own. It's far enough from the highway you have to know what you're looking for to find it.

"How come I've never been here?"

"I guess no one ever showed it to you."

"Maybe," she says, and scrambles down the bank to the water's edge. We walk along the creek, making a new trail through the grass. Cottonwoods overhead. Unseen birds in the branches.

I see three small brown trout in the shadow of a fallen log. I point to them but Lucy can't pick them out.

"What do you say we go get a burger and a beer at the Union?" I say. "It's Sunday. We don't have anywhere to be."

"I was kind of hoping you weren't going to say we should go to town, but I am starting to get hungry."

"Let's do it."

The ride to town is quiet. Pleasant. After we park Lucy stops on the sidewalk and looks around. There are few rough-looking trucks by the bar, and a couple more cars down at the Pizza Hut, but the rest of the street is empty, still.

"Are we really going in there?" she asks.

"Just keep your head down. You'll be fine."

"If I get recognized it's all your fault."

Inside, the bar smells like fried onion

rings and human breath. It's lively enough for the time of day. Blake Shelton on the stereo. We sit down next to the Megatouch machine. Lucy gives the place a quick glance over. She puts her elbows on the bar and says in a low voice "I forgot how all the guys wear hats to the bar here. What am I doing here? What are we doing here?"

"We live here now, right?"

"You might," she says, narrowing her eyes then putting her hands on her chest. "I never said that."

"I'm looking around and I know three people in this bar. One's my cousin. That guy over there." I nod to the scrawny, gray-faced man in the hooded sweatshirt under the TV. "But he wouldn't come talk to me. Our families don't speak."

"Do you think you can stand it?" Lucy asks in almost a whisper. "Actually living here? I'm pretty sure you and I have always felt the same way about this place."

The bartender comes and neither of us is feeling too hungry. We order Crown and Cokes.

"That was before I left," I say. "There's

something awful about trying to build a life in a place where you don't belong, where the natives don't want you around."

"That's not how I think of it. Just because you're from some place doesn't make it yours."

"Tell that to the people in this bar."

As soon as we have our drinks we go out on the back patio to share one of Lucy's rolled cigarettes.

"So what was California like?"

"At least you want to know," I say. "Most people here don't seem interested." I look out at the pale blue sky. "It does feel better having someone like you here."

She takes a drag of her cigarette, kicks the toe of her boot against the floor, holds the stir stick aside with her finger to take a drink.

"Sorry," I say. "That was awkward."

"So why do you want to be a journalist?"

"Who told you I wanted to be a journalist?"

"Isn't that what you're doing? Working for the paper?"

"I want to be a writer. Even if that feels

weird to say."

"If it feels weird then maybe it's not right for you. Shouldn't you be more confident than that?"

"Maybe."

"What kind of a writer do you want to be?"

"A good one."

"No, I mean, poet or —?

"A novelist."

"Hmm," she says and finishes her drink in one shot. "Don't good writers need more experiences? You need to travel more. Do you even have a passport?"

"Jesus. No. You're right about that. But I want to write about this place first."

"Winterborn? Who's going to read that? Are you ready to go back yet?"

I drive out of town with the radio off, the car quiet, the road empty.

"We do live in pretty amazing times," she says. "To be moving across the ground at 70 miles an hour. To have air conditioning."

"We're basically on the Oregon Trail right now. Not that long ago people were killing bison to stay alive right over there." I point to the silver ribbon of the North Platte River.

"And now we just turn up the music and go," she says.

"Just keep going until we either hit the city or one of the coasts."

"I'd settle for a mountain."

"So would I."

At her driveway I slow down to a crawl and gently make the turn.

"You don't have to do that. We're not sixteen anymore."

"Sorry. Old habit. Don't want to get in trouble for keeping you out too long."

She gets out and comes around to my window.

"This was fun," she says. "Kinda." She wags her fingers in a cute little wave as she walks away. I try to be stoic so I put the truck in drive without watching her go inside.

The land spreads out in the brown and gold of fallow fields. The air sharp, the sky clear. Only a little wind. I can see south to the ridgeline. The eroding finger of stone to the east and the monument to the west. The valley still, paused until planting season. I stand out on the deck oiling the trap launcher. In my black wool hat and overalls I look like a German-from-Russia immigrant from the Old World. Out here I'm all right with that. Carrick drives into the yard, parks, and lifts his gun from the back of the truck.

"Perfect day for killing some clay pigeons," I say as he walks up.

A .410 and a 12 gauge lean against the side of the house. Boxes of shells next to the launcher. We load up the guns, the ammo, the launcher and a cooler of beer on the back of the Mule. Drive out to the beet field.

I hand Carrick a cold silver can of beer and load up the pedal launcher with blue rock. We each take a side. Carrick calls "pull" and I stomp the pedal and the targets soar. Carrick tracks the diminishing shape for an instant before firing the small bore .410.

"Dammit," he says.

"You're going to have to be a pretty good shot with that little thing," I say.

"I'll get it. Don't worry."

After two boxes we're both clearing our sides every time. The sound from the guns carries for miles on that quiet day.

Shoulders sore, ears ringing, we sit on the tailgate and open our second beer.

"So is it good to be back?" Carrick asks.

I look at him and take a swig.

"Ask me in a year, or in five years. Right now it feels pretty good to be here. To be around people I know. On land I know," I open my arms to the empty fields. "This, what we're doing right now, where else could you and I have access to the land to do it?"

"I think it's all about managing your expectations," Carrick says, staring out at the horizon.

"Oh fuck. Don't give me that." I shake my head and take another drink.

"I hated myself as soon as I said that, but, I mean, it is. You have to know where you are."

"I know where I am." I look up. Three jets, two traveling west, one traveling east, streak the gray with white contrails. "And I know where I'm not."

Carrick jumps up and fires a shot into the sky.

"Like I said, you're going to need a bigger gun. Oh, I forgot, I brought something else for us to shoot."

In the glove compartment of the Mule is a .45 caliber Kimber pistol. I hand it to Carrick. He unrolls a Denver Broncos poster and pins it to the end of the hay bale. We take turns, each going through a clip. The gun kicks and booms like a bomb going off with each shot. In no time, the starting squad from 2002 is in tatters.

When we're finished, shells litter the ground. Carrick goes over to the bale and sets the poster on fire with his lighter. The dry hay goes up in a blaze.

"What the fuck are you doing?" I ask.

"Burning the evidence. What's it look like?"

"No, seriously. Why'd you do that?"

"You can't feed that to cows, can you? It'll break their teeth, right? With all the bullets in it?"

"Man, I didn't realize you were such a city boy. We just shot that with a .45 caliber handgun from 20 yards. There's no way any of those bullets are still in there."

The bale flares up and we stand there watching it burn, the smoke drifting up toward the contrails.

My phone rings throughout the day on Monday. Concerned citizens. Falconer's neighboring landowners. Readers wanting to know about the next meeting. I also take a call from a representative from Raptor, a guy named Joe, corporate counsel.

"Why the hit piece?" he asks. His speech is clipped, his tone one of irritation.

"Do you consider that a hit piece?"

"We do. I would advise you to back off the corporate-history-presented-as-facts just because it was printed in another newspaper."

"Were any of my facts wrong?"

"We feel they were presented in a very one-sided way."

"I'd be happy to hear your side."

"Our side at Raptor is that we would rather you didn't write about us at all."

"I'm probably not going to do that. Would you like to speak with my editor?"

"We've gone through this before in other communities. Several times. If this keeps going we're going to have to speak to your publisher.

"I'm fine with that as well."

"Not a threat. I just want you to understand where we're coming from."

When the call ends Jerry looks over, smiling. "What was that?" he asks. I want to tell him to mind his own business, but instead I ignore him and go to Guy's office.

"Just a heads up," I say. Guy holds up one finger indicating he needs a second to finish a thought. He turns to me with a fairly severe look on his face, eyebrows raised. I clear my throat and continue. "A lawyer from Raptor just called and vaguely threatened me."

"What do you mean by 'vaguely?'"

"He said we need to stop writing about his company."

"Or what?"

"Or he's going to talk to Charles."

"Did he say our story was inaccurate?"

"No."

"Did he have any problem with our facts?"

"No."

"Then he's grasping at straws. Typical bullshit intimidation tactics. He's just trying to silence you, which means that you're probably onto a good story. If he calls back and tries that again you can send him to me."

"Got it. Thanks for the support."

"That's what I do."

A group of landowners and concerned citizens form a group called Save Our Underground Lifeblood (SOUL). SOUL hosts another meeting in Arikaree, this time at the VFW. I attend and write about it for the paper. This story is mine now. I field phone calls at the office about wastewater. Read through the relevant letters to the editor, of which we're getting at least two a day now, to ensure their accuracy. And read up as much as I can on fracking and the environmental impacts of wastewater injection wells.

The next weekend, Lucy calls to ask if I'm busy. Would I want to come over and work cattle with her? Why not? I could use a day of being outside and getting dirty.

"Sure," I say. "I'll be there. Just let me get my stuff together."

I put on work jeans and a pair of cowboy boots I never wear and head over to her house. It's just after dawn and the sky is cloudless, dim, cold.

Lucy drives down to the feedlot to pick up the trailers, horses and an ATV. She has a thermos of coffee for each of us. I can manage on a horse but I'm no cowboy, so I take a camouflaged Yamaha four-wheeler and ride in the back, following the bulls at a distance.

The cattle trudge along over the prairie grass in a shapeless herd, guided by the horses on the flanks and me pushing up from the rear. A bull stops and looks back at me, feigning to break from the rest. A young one, a two-year-old, with all the heat and courage he would ever have. Steam rising from the crest of his hump. He looks out past us at the land he thinks he could roam if he could get free. Before he can fully turn away I'm there with the ATV, revving the engine, pushing him back until he's absorbed into the plodding black mass.

With all the bulls corralled, my next job is to drive a pickup and cattle trailer. I've been asked to take a few bulls at a time out to separate herds in the far reaches of the pasture. The aim is to disperse the big beasts to their own harem of cows for breeding. When I back the trailer gate up to the corral chute the cowboys who live on the ranch show patience with my driving skills.

"Pull forward. Straighten it out," the one called Chris says. "You got it."

I watch from the side mirrors as Chris directs me. As I close on the chute, the cowboy holds his hands out in front of him like he's compressing an imaginary basketball, slowly collapsing it until the trailer comes flush with the corral. The crew pushes a half dozen bulls onto the trailer. Each one shakes the gooseneck and the cab of the truck when it rushes on.

Lucy jumps in with me on my third trip out.

"You're doing really well," she says. "I'm impressed. I think everyone is. I didn't think you could cut it."

"This cowboy stuff is nothing," I say. "No sweat."

"I won't tell anyone you said that."

"No, seriously. I was freaking out for a while. I'm still nervous when those guys are watching. But this is great. Thank you for inviting me. This place, this piece of land we're on, is incredible. I'd love to come out here and just write."

"Write?"

"Work on something. It's so peaceful."

She laughs a full-throated laugh. "Yeah right," she says. "That's not going to happen."

We look out through the dirty windshield of the flatbed Ford truck over dewy prairie grass, subtle ripples in the geology, the sky a gray hue and getting more blue as the day heats up. The odor of sagebrush and dust. Cowboys chattering on the CB. A few quick whistles from a meadowlark. Then we come upon a small pond. Cattails emerging along the edges. The water smooth, undisturbed. The pasture road narrows as we drive around it. I slow and Lucy rolls down the window.

"Look at that," she says.

A flock of pelicans glides over the water in formation, rising and falling single file as if roped together from beak to tail feathers. Silent. Smooth. A graceful wonder.

As I'm marveling the outside wheel of the dual-axle trailer drops off the edge of the road and strikes the cement culvert that runs from the pond to the pasture. The tire peels away from the rim of the wheel, dead flat. I stop.

"Goddammit," I say. I step out of the truck. "That was about as stupid as I've been in a while." I check the back of the truck. No jack, only a small toolbox with some rusted wrenches. "I can't fix this with these."

Lucy grabs the CB.

"Mayday, mayday," she says, looking at me.

"Shit. Don't do that," I say.

"Charlie Chaplin, do you copy?"

"This is Charlie," comes in with a squawk.

"We have a little problem here. Need assistance. Over."

"10-4. What's your 20?"

"West side of the north pond. Over."

"10-4. On my way. Over."

We sit on the bed of the truck and wait, quiet, looking for dust on the horizon. We see the small cloud before we see the white flatbed approaching.

Chris takes a steel ramp off the back and lays it in front of the good trailer tire.

"Looks like you had some bad luck," he says. "Pull ahead and we'll get this up there."

I jump in the truck and slowly drive forward until the good tire rolls up onto the ramp. Chris cranks on the tire iron but the nuts are too rusted to turn alone. We pull together until we pop them all loose.

By the time we switch the tire out we're both sweating and dirty.

"Bad thing is you didn't have very far to

go," Chris says.

"Appreciate your help," I say.

Lucy gets in and we drive on.

"This cowboy stuff's no sweat, huh?" Lucy says.

"Fucking pelicans."

I come as close to the herd as I can, stop, and open the back gate. Three of the black, two-thousand-pound creatures bound from the trailer and trot off toward the cows.

"Jealous of those guys," I say.

"You would be."

A few more trips like that and we finish the day and go back for dinner. I'm scraping off my boots on a metal plate embedded in the cement by the front door when I see the tail of a rattlesnake disappear into the grass. I'm tired. Pretty sure I'll be sore tomorrow, and I haven't felt better in a long time.

On the drive out to my house she takes pictures with her phone, posts them, and smiles to herself. The fields have been planted and the weeds in the barrow pits are turning green. When we pull into my driveway she gives me a half smile.

"So this is your place," she says.

A few pine trees stand around the white house. The red deck paint peels but the wood's good. Chipped white paint on the outbuildings — a barn, pump house, and garage. What's left of the corral sags in disrepair.

"What are we doing now?" she asks and spreads out her arms.

"We should have a toast," I say. I bring down a bottle of cabernet sauvignon from on top of the fridge. After peeling off the orange discount sticker, $4.99, I open the wine and let it breathe. She picks up the bottle and inspects the label. "Black Swan. Hmm...never heard of it. Do we need to decant it?"

"Probably. But we don't have any decanters out here. We just drink it."

I wipe out two wine glasses with a paper towel and pour. She swirls the wine and smells it.

"Black cherry. Vanilla. A little bit of oak," she says.

I sniff my glass. "Wine. Wine. A little bit of wine."

"Oh, don't give me that. Has the country made you simple overnight? I know you're more sophisticated than you let on."

I approach her by the counter. We each take another sip of wine and kiss and I go to my knees.

"Not here," she says.

In the bedroom she smells of lavender and soap.

We're still half-dressed and have just returned to our wine in the kitchen when the front door opens. Lucy runs back to the bedroom.

"What do you think this is? Your local bar?" I ask, in my underwear, holding my glass up to Carrick, who isn't smiling.

"Good god," he says. "Put some clothes on. I don't want to see something I'll never be able to unsee."

He saunters into the living room, plugs his phone into the speakers and puts on a dead country singer who croons about changing his life.

Lucy comes out of the bathroom and introduces herself to Carrick.

"I remember you," Carrick says. "Cheers." He hits his glass hard against Lucy's then finishes his gin. "So why'd you come back?"

"That's a good question."

Seeing she isn't going to elaborate, he continues. "I don't really bring this up too much. People here tend to think it sounds like bragging. But you've at least been somewhere. I used to live in New York. Before I blew up my life here, left, then came back. I miss it. Especially in the summer. The concerts in the parks. Bike riding at night. And the bars. Fuck. That city has the best bars."

"You should go back. Why not?"

"Yeah, right," Carrick says. "You'll never hear me talk about leaving again. I know better."

"Such a realist," I say. "Hey Carrick, come outside. I have something I want to show you. We'll be right back."

I walk ahead out to the barn. Inside I hand Carrick a lighter and a little one-hitter with some Colorado marijuana packed in the tip.

"Dude," I say. "Can I ask you a favor? Try not to blow this for me. We might not be perfect for each other, but we get along pretty well together. And I'm competing with the whole immense fucking outside world. She could leave at any time. So try to be on my side, if you can."

Carrick chuckles as he blows out his hit. "Good luck. You know it can suck here. This can be a dark place. We both know that."

"It can be if you let it. But it's also not that bad. I really think if we can make it work Lucy and I could build a good life together here. Buy a house. Have a garden. Get a dog. Maybe raise a family at some point. And we have good friends here. You're one of them. But I need you to be on your best behavior, at least while she's out here. Can you do that for me?"

"Shit, man. That's serious. But I'm not going to lie, if that's what you're asking me to do. I'm going to be who I always am."

"C'mon, dude. Did you see her? She's hot. Smart. We get along really well."

"I'll tell you what. We'll see how tonight goes and if I like her then I'll do what you want."

"You're an asshole."

"What do you want me to say? I'm not trying to change anybody. Don't try it with me."

"Let's go inside. Try not to drink too much."

"Saying shit like that only makes me drink more. You should know that by now."

"Sweet friend you are."

"Hey. You're the one getting dark. I'm just telling the truth."

We go in and Lucy shows Carrick pictures of her old apartment on her phone.

"Put that away," I say. "No more city talk.

Winterborn is where it's at. Back to the land. The new hipster Mecca. There's nothing more subversive than moving to the middle of nowhere."

"Right. More like you can check out, but you can never leave," Carrick says.

We order take-out from the Mexican restaurant on the edge of town. Carrick and I go in to pick it up.

"You can't kiss her ass into staying here," Carrick says. "People can't be persuaded like that. Think of it this way. Have you ever been pulled over?"

"That's a stupid question."

"Right, so you know how a cop comes up to you and he either gives you a warning or a fine. He asks you questions like 'do you know how fast you were going?' And you try to talk him into not giving you a ticket, either acting clueless or being honest or lying about the size of your tires or something. But nothing you say means anything. He already knows whether or not he's giving you a ticket the moment he opens his door to walk up to you. You can't talk your way out of it. This chick knows if she's going to stay. Sure. Treat her right. Take care of her. Have a good time. But you're not going to make up your mind for her."

"You give awful advice."

After we eat and Carrick leaves we lay in my bed, the distance between us cold. I try to cross it.

"What's going on in that head of yours?" I ask

"Carrick's nicer than I remember. He misses New York so much. I don't blame him."

"People love to talk about far away places, don't they?"

"True. You should hear my friends talk about Idaho. And Montana. Like they're these wonderlands of nature and wild things. Like they're other planets."

"We're not that far away from either of those places. We could go tomorrow."

"They're still pretty far away."

"They're not, really. That's one of the nice things about living here."

"Stop trying to get me to like it here. I know what you're doing."

We lay there listening to the train pass

down in the river valley.

"It's so small here," she says. "So isolat-ed."

Short bursts from the whistle.

"Nowhere," she says.

Then the big quiet.

The day the earth moves I'm in the office working on a story about a girl who has been mauled by a pack of wild dogs on the Indian reservation just across the border in South Dakota.

My phone rings: Mary Winslow.

"It finally happened," she says.

"What was that, ma'am?"

"They pumped in enough wastewater to shake the ground."

"How do you mean?"

"I mean we just had our first earthquake."

"Really? I don't think we felt anything here."

"Well we sure did."

"Can you tell me what happened?"

"Didn't last long, but we felt it."

"OK. Thank you. I'll see what I can find out. Can I give you a call later if I need to get some more details?"

"Sure. We all knew this was going to happen and they went ahead and did it anyway. Come up and I'll show you."

First, I pull up the U.S. Geological Survey's website and find the map of recent earthquakes. Just as Mary said, there's an orange dot with 3.2 next to it north of Arikaree. Now I know I'm on a big story. Western Nebraska doesn't get earthquakes.

Mary lives in a bungalow north of town. A squat brick house with a red door and white trim. She says she's from Ohio but by the way her yard looks she might as well be from Arizona. Xeriscaping, I recall, is the name for yards with rocks in place of grass. I notice multiple hummingbird feeders on the railing of the front porch and pots with short cacti near the door. I knock, and after a couple of minutes Mary appears, more substantial than I would have thought from her frail phone voice.

"Oh dear, you came," she says. "Come in. Hope you don't mind cats."

"Actually I'm allergic."

"Well I'll come out there then," she says. "I just wanted you to come up here so you could see something."

She takes us behind the house to a patch of dead grass with an old stone well. "Now come look at this," she says. "See here how the stones are cracked around the one side. That wasn't like that yesterday. I was out here hanging clothes up and it was fine."

I photograph the cracked stones and write down her account — swinging lights and a plate that fell off the wall — then go out to the wastewater injection site. Since I had scoped it out last the company had put up another fence closer to the highway with Keep Out and No Trespassing signs. I take pictures of those as well then return to the office to make a few more phone calls and write my story.

I learn from calling around that the oil and gas commission has installed a "stoplight system" on Falconer's injection well. Green means little to no seismicity so inject away, orange the seismic pressure is building so slow down the injecting, and red means stop.

Raptor ran the red light and Arikaree felt two tremors — 3.2 and 4.1 — and the subsequent aftershocks. Strong enough to crack the foundation of the Methodist church and open up a seam in the bank of the Tri-State irrigation canal north of town.

A day later a truck full of wastewater breaks an axle and spills its contents on the side of the road near the entrance to the site. The ground there quickly takes on a gray hue. The weeds and grass die in a few days.

So the dam bursts for negative public sentiment toward the injection well. Letters to the editor pour in. My day-to-day work becomes covering county commission and city council meetings along with the oil and gas commission hearings. The main complaint and worry is over the aquifer. Citizens educate themselves on the intricacies of the underground water source. They also learn the toxins in the wastewater down to each separate chemical and its parts per million.

I begin to recognize the regulars at the protests and meetings and they soon know me. We become familiar enough that our chummy conversation makes me slightly uncomfortable. Personally I admire them for taking the fight to the oilmen, but I can't be seen as favorable to any one side in my coverage.

The big paper from Omaha sends out their statewide correspondent to cover the hearings. Activists who have been mobilized by a fight over an oil pipeline in eastern Nebraska bring their protest experience and know-how with fighting government regulators to Winterborn. The story isn't likely to go national, but this is as close as the people of the Panhandle can hope for.

Early one morning Charles comes over to my desk holding a copy of the Omaha paper.

"Says here the commission wants to review its rules for how much water can be injected in one day."

"That's in my story," I say.

"Is it?"

"After the jump. We led with the comments from the lady in Arikaree who said a vase fell off her shelf during the last earthquake and nearly killed her Shih-Tzu. Omaha didn't have that."

"Maybe they did but didn't think it was

important."

"It was an interesting anecdote."

"Let me ask you this: Do you think you have enough experience to be writing about this?"

"Guy seems fine with how this is going."

"Let me take it up with him. We need to be writing about the hard news. Not the stories every old lady with a dog tells us."

Once the Omaha reporter turns his attention to the story I see the difference between working for a small town paper and a metro daily. The city reporter can get access — people call him back, speak on the record — when I'm dismissed, ignored. But the city reporter doesn't know the people like we do, and they open up to me with the details of their lives — the vase-on-dog story just one instance — in a candid way that's exclusive to my reporting. Guy guides me to double-down on those stories. Go to their homes, he says. Find out how these earthquakes and constant truck traffic impact their lives, their mental health, their quality of life. The stories do well and I'm thanked by members of the community for my reporting. I'm learning

that it's hard to compete with personal emo-
tion when it comes to telling a good story.

My phone rings at 6 a.m. on a Sunday.

"Hey, if you're not doing anything, do you think you could help me out?" Lucy asks.

"Possibly."

"No pelicans this time."

"Then I'm in."

She waits for me on the deck of the farm-house. Hands me a thermos of coffee when we get in her truck. We drive south across the grasslands toward Colorado. This part of Colorado is Nebraska just as the bordering part of Kansas is Nebraska and vice versa. All the same type of land. Once it was all prairie. All sea of grass. The farm we arrive at, the estate auction remnants could have been a sale in my county, even down the road from Lucy's farm.

I used to understand this way of life down to the rusted nuts and bolts on the half-buried-in-weeds farm equipment. Or at least I did until my family quit farming. Now I'm not so sure I feel as though I belong out in the country. Tractors have become self-driving, guided by satellites, and farmers take on more land than we would have dreamed of farming. The game has changed, and as much as I want to stay connected to the world that I came from, I've stepped out of line and it's passing me by.

Am I OK with that? I don't know. I know I'm not trying to buy land to become a farmer. But still I envy the man who makes his money growing food, of a life spent outdoors, of a livelihood that depends on instincts and ingenuity to succeed. I could never go back to it, but part of me mourns the loss of a way of life that had been in my family for generations. At least today I'll reconnect with what I grew up learning.

Out in the yard sits the same white Case tractors from the '70s and early '80s bought when the market was strong, the same type of rusting field equipment — discs and rougheners to keep the dust down when it won't rain.

"That's you over there," Lucy says, pointing toward an '80s model Case 2390 tractor, white with orange wheels, the decals peeling off the cab, a loader on the front end, hooked up to a grain cart. "My dad bought this last week and we need to get it home. You know these things a lot better than I do. I need you to drive it back. Did you pay attention to how we got here?"

I get in and it's like some kind of built-in instinct takes over from summers spent in similar machines. I fire it up and drive it out of the junkyard and onto the road. The tractor bucks as I shift up into road gear. The thrill quickly fades when it tops out at 18 miles per hour. The landscape rolls by like a slowed down movie reel. I pass more abandoned farmhouses than working farms.

When I arrive at the interstate I can see the oncoming traffic fine but once I pull onto the shoulder of the highway I realize the grain cart is too large, wider than my side mirrors and taller than the rearview. I can't see behind me at all. I'm traveling less than

20 miles per hour down an interstate with cars and trucks passing at 70 to 80 mph and I'm blind to what's coming up on me.

Then at the fork in the road I have to get on the left tine going west. I switch on the blinker, which I'm fairly certain can't be seen from behind, and attempt the lane change. As I try to turn the wheel a tractor-trailer appears inches away. I pull back into my lane and take a breath. The exit rolls closer. I veer to the side to take a look at the traffic coming up behind me. I can only see about a quarter mile before the road drops down a hill. I wait for the highway to clear then cross. A few cars pass, another semi, then I go for it. Throttle up. Slam the gear shift forward, the tractor jerking, the pin hitch rattling as the grain cart bucks. I'm about halfway across when I hear the horn from an approaching semi. I hold my line and just as I cross into the left lane and make an exit I see a speeding mass of steel flash by on my right and take the lane going east.

As I crest the exit ramp I look down on the other highway. The truck has stopped on the side of the road and the driver is out and hollering and kicking the dirt.

I drive on. After a few miles the engine overheats and steam comes pouring out of the radiator. The metaphor so obvious it's a cliche. I slow to let it cool and continue on at half throttle.

When I make it back to Lucy's place hours later she's sitting on the deck smoking. I park the tractor in the middle of the drive- way, get out and without looking at her walk to my truck.

"What took so long?" she says, standing up, smiling. "Did you have some trouble? Were you looking at pelicans again?"

"That was terrible," I say. "Stupidest thing I ever did."

"What happened?"

She reaches into cooler next to her and comes as close as she can to hand it to me. The beer's good and cold. I tell her.

"Sounds like you had some bad luck," she says. "But you passed that test."

After a day of phone calls from upset subscribers, Jerry being Jerry, hateful internet comments, Guy asks me if he can buy me dinner. He wants to go to Prime Cut. Monday's salmon night.

"The only place in town we can get decent seafood," he says. "Here and the Country Club. But they don't like me too much up there. Just the way I want it."

At the restaurant with vinyl booths, dim lights and original decor from the '50s, I fork up a piece of pale salmon next to a medley of cooked vegetables. Guy dips a fried shrimp into cocktail sauce.

"By the way, it's obvious you're trying to figure this job out," he says. "You're still really green, but you're coming along."

"Thanks. I know I have a lot to learn about news writing."

"I think you're going to get there. What I like about you is that you're from here, and keeping you around would be good for the community. I could see you building a life in Winterborn."

"If newspapers can survive."

"They'll still be around. They might not look how they look now, but towns will always need their news. I mean, look at the work we're doing on wastewater. The only way people find out anything about that is through solid reporting."

"Speaking of that, don't look now, but I think Dale Falconer just walked in."

The rancher walks in with his wife, a straight-haired blonde in Wranglers and a jean jacket. The hostess sits them at a booth across the aisle and two tables down from us. Falconer has his back to us but his wife recognizes me and says something to her husband. Falconer turns, looks us over, then approaches.

"You guys selling any papers?" Falconer asks. Guy sets his fork down and looks at him. "You think maybe if you put more of my business in the paper you'll sell a few more?"

"Guy, this is Dale Falconer," I say. "Dale, Guy's my boss."

"I know that," the rancher says. "This is who's giving you more rope than you need. Probably just enough to hang yourself with."

"Can we help you with something?" Guy asks.

"You could start by keeping my name out of the paper."

"All right," Guy says, sitting back, clearly comfortable in the situation. "Let me ask you this. If I drove over to your ranch and tried telling you how to raise cattle what would you do?"

"If I ever see either of you on my property you'll meet the business end of my shotgun."

"You're missing the point. You wouldn't want a newspaperman telling you how to ranch. And I don't appreciate you telling me how to do my job. I've been in the newspaper business for a long time."

"Seems to me you still have plenty to learn."

"We're trying to have dinner here. You should get back to your wife."

Falconer turns to me.

"What do your parents think about what you're doing?"

"I mean, they don't live here. But they read the paper online. They seem proud enough if that's what you're asking."

"Do they? I wonder how they'd like it if someone started printing their business on the front page of the paper. They probably wouldn't be so proud then."

"What's this really about?" Guy asks. "Have we gotten anything wrong?"

"This whole thing is wrong. Do you know someone put a dead skunk in our mailbox?"

"I didn't know that," Guy says. "Do you have pictures? Can we get you to tell us what happened on the record?"

"Hell no. You reporters make me sick," Falconer nearly spits. "You're parasites. Living off what other people do."

Guy slides out of the booth and stands up.

"That's about enough," he says. "You need to get going. We're trying to eat here."

Falconer squares off with Guy and as soon as they start to lean toward each other Falconer's wife has a grip on his arm. "C'mon, Dale. Let's go somewhere else," she says.

"Just keep my goddamn name out of the paper," Falconer says.

"Just don't screw up and we will," Guy says.

Falconer and his wife walk past their table and out of the restaurant.

Guy sits and grins.

"That was fun. The guy was upset. That's how you know you've got the bastards."

My sides are twitching and my palms sweaty. But Guy's amusement calms me some. I wonder if I'll ever get that calloused.

"You're a little rattled," he says. "I can see that. You'll get a thicker skin. You'll have to if you're going to make it in this business."

"I have a 10 a.m. phone call with Mr. Robey," I say.

"Putting you through."

The numbing drone of Muzak for several minutes.

"Yes?"

"Mr. Robey. This is Ethan Thomas with the Sun-Gazette."

"Right. The so-called reporter."

"Excuse me?"

"Do you have some questions so we can get this done? At least one of us is very busy."

"What can you say about the earthquake north of Arikaree?"

"Alleged earthquake. You do know that the science of seismology is far from perfect. More theories and guesswork than actual science."

"So you're denying that there was an earthquake."

"I'm saying consider the source of your alleged facts."

I question the CEO of Raptor about the wastewater injection, starting by asking how many gallons they're dumping:

"No comment. I don't want to advertise for my competition."

How many trucks:

"Not enough. We're fracking as fast as we can in Colorado but there's a lot more oil to get to."

The potential for spills:

"No safer way to do this known to man."

What happens in the event of an accident:

"Have you heard of something called insurance?"

The risk to the aquifer:

"Overblown. We're injecting water a mile down past the groundwater. Do you know what would have to happen for any of that water to escape? The layer we're dumping into is enormous, infinitely expanding. We could dump millions of gallons of water into it for years and never fill it up."

Anything else you'd like to add:

"Just this. Fracking is safe. Wastewater injection is safe. And the people of western Nebraska have nothing to be concerned about."

I thank the man for his time then start work on the story.

Again, it's published on page 1.

When I get to her house she's sitting on the back deck talking on the phone. Since I saw her last she has cut her hair short and it's back to her original color — black. She looks like a raven, a creature that could pick up and fly away at a moment's notice. I walk up and she smiles as she talks to a friend in another city. I wait, trying not to listen to her as she speaks in her slightly raspy, mirthful voice. The sun falls below the horizon behind the bluff on the far side of the valley.

I watch as a lone firefly blinks in the tall grass next to the barbed wire fence. Birds in the cottonwoods along the road. I can hear the coal train running down along the river.

Its horn sends waves of sound out over the land, breaking over us. I wait.

When she finishes the call she sits looking out over the valley, smiling. I get in the truck and she makes me wait some more before she joins me. She hands me a water bottle full of cold, dark brown sun tea. I drive down over the river, through the two little towns. We're talking about tornadoes and she looks out the window quiet, coolly taking it in. We pass an underground missile silo with a tall chainlink fence and a blinking red light. I turn at the next road and drive into a lot that's been cleared for gravel mining. Park alongside a brokedown truck and get out.

I lead up through the pasture. The drought is in its fifth year and there are few flying insects, just our feet making tufts of dust in the shrubs. The breeze carries on it the sweet smell of the prairie. We hike to the base of the exposed sandstone and sit on a patch of grass.

From up there we can hear the dim white noise of the missile silo humming below. Yellow dots from ranch yardlights speck the dark land. We can see the edge of the valley dozens of miles away, and below it the cluster of lights that make up the town.

"This is one of my favorite places on the planet," I say. "The kind of place I'll keep with me my whole life. The kind of place that you'd only know about if you lived here. You'd never find this living in a new city."

"Maybe," she says.

"How many places do you know like this in the world? A handful? And how often will you visit them before you die? Maybe a dozen. Maybe less. This might be the last time I ever come here."

"You fancy yourself something of a philosopher, do you?" she says, and puts her arm in mine. "Just try to enjoy the view."

I laugh and look out over the land, all the space that can be taken in by the eye. I lean in closer to her and when my face is close she pulls back.

"This place is so empty," she says. "A barren wasteland. Have you ever been to the Pacific Northwest? Not that long ago I was living in the forest, in a neighborhood where the trees are taller than the buildings. Everything green. Everything alive. So much more life there."

"Everything's alive around us here," I say. "The grass is expanding at our feet. The air is a swirling mixture of gases. The light you see is traveling through space to get to your eyes. What you can't see is also there."

"Then why does it all feel so dead? So static. So sad. So empty."

"Use your imagination."

"Are you serious?"

"Anyone can love the ocean, or the mountains. Loving this requires a little more effort. Maybe you were born at the wrong time to be living in a place like this."

"And born at the right time to live someplace else."

We quiet down and look out across the prairie.

"You can't do that," she says. "You can't stop talking. I can't handle the silence."

Across the valley three lightning bolts strike the top of the biggest bluff. Then the stampeding hoof clatter of distant thunder.

"There's a little noise for you," I say. "It's a bull running off a trailer. A ten thousand buffalo soundbyte."

A storm cloud smudges the stars and sky into a deep gray as it drifts toward us. Lightning webs the higher clouds like the circuitry of an electrified destroyer. Bolts spark from the hull to the ground.

"It's a ghost ship," she says. "Let's get off this bluff before it torpedoes us."

The rain hits just as we're getting in the car. It comes down heavy, rushed, desperate. The sky flashes as we drive the dirt roads back to her place, the road noise louder in the truck from the mud on the tires hitting the undercarriage.

"God that rain smells good," she says.

The quiet returns stronger than before. I see the green lights of horses' eyes glinting by the roadside. This is her family's land. I slow the truck and roll down my window. The instant the wheels stop spinning she's out of the truck and at the fence.

She places a hand on the neck of the brown mare with a star on her head, Lucy's horse. One of the others, a tall, blaze-faced bay gelding approaches me with nostrils pumping to catch my scent. Heat and energy crackles around them as though they've been electrically charged.

"I'll probably see you later," she says. "Maybe tomorrow. Maybe in a few days. Maybe not."

She steps up on the fence as the mare comes aside. She mounts and they lope off into the dark.

Charles slinks over while I'm writing a 10-inch story on Habitat for Humanity's biggest home build to date. He doesn't say anything until I feel him staring and look up.

"Jesus," I say. "How long have you been standing there?"

"Just observing," he says in his drawl.

"Can I help you?"

"The CEO of Raptor is coming by in an hour. He wouldn't tell me what it's about, just that he's coming and he wants you and Guy there. 4 p.m. Conference room."

Before I can respond that I'll be there, Charles walks away. I peer out over the other monitors in the open newsroom, keeping an eye on the door until in walk two men, both clean shaven and skinny, wearing puffy coats from an outdoor lifestyle company that men in this community would never wear. The only acceptable outdoor leisure wear in Winterborn is either for hunting or fishing, and neither call for shiny lightweight down jackets. Clearly Colorado men.

The receptionist heads them off then directs them to the conference room.

I stop by Guy's office. He's filed his editorial for the day and looks satisfied and relaxed behind his desk, leaning back in his chair with his hands behind his head. I hate to disrupt his peace.

"You're not going to like this but the oil guys are here and they want to talk to us."

"Oh goodie." He sighs as he stands.

We sit around a long wooden table and Guy positions himself as far away from the puffy coats as possible.

"So," Charles says. "What can we do for you gentlemen?"

"Well, you could start by printing the facts," the man with freckles and reddish hair, Robey, says. "Your cub reporter here seems mighty inexperienced."

"What facts would you like us to print

that we haven't already?" Guy asks.

"I'm the one who was interviewed, and I think your kid here exaggerated what I said."

"That's a pretty serious charge," Guy says. "What exactly are you referring to?"

He calls up a document on his phone and reads: "On Monday, Ethan Thomas wrote, in a quote attributed to me, 'the layer we're dumping into is enormous, infinitely expanding.' Now your kid here knows whether or not I really said that, and he's going to have to make up his own mind whether that's the truth, but I know I never said it. Because I know I'd never be that dumb to say something that inflammatory, that could be misconstrued by the public."

"I'm certain you said that, sir," I say. "I can go get my notes."

"That's not necessary," Guy says. "I've already written more inflammatory statements than that on the editorial page. Let me ask you guys this. Did you ever stop to think how it would look when you decided to bring your dirty Colorado water up here to dump it in Nebraska? Did it ever occur to you that we're not your dumping ground? Not your landfill?"

"Let me ask you this," Robey says. "How did you get to work today? You drove. That pen in your hand — it's plastic. Where does plastic come from? Do you realize how much of your life is made possible because of oil?"

"Has anyone here said we're against oil?" Guy asks. "We just don't think we should have to take your toxic waste."

"If you want oil you're going to have to deal with the cleanup."

"Not here we don't. And not from an out-of-state company."

"What we're doing isn't illegal."

"It oughta be."

"Might I suggest you at least put one of your more seasoned journalists on this, if you have one. I know it's hard to find good help when you can't pay your reporters anything."

"Ethan grew up here, and he knows this land better than anyone in this room. Like me, he doesn't want you to ruin it either."

"I appreciate that sentiment. But that's all it is — sentiment. You guys are trying to be objective, right?"

"We're trying to tell the truth," Guy says.

"Well, hey now, let's not get too

high-minded," Charles says. "We all know there's always more than one truth."

Guy doesn't look at him.

"That's right," Robey says. "I would advise you to make sure you choose the right one to tell."

"That's about enough intimidation for one day," Guy says. "Some of us have to work for a living. You guys know where the door is. Try not to spill anything on your way back to Colorado." He stands and offers his hand. No takers. "But let's keep in touch. I'm sure we'll be calling you after the next earthquake or other preventable man-made disaster."

"And our lawyers will be calling if you print anything that's not factual."

"Fine with me," Guy says.

I come home after a day of reporting, processing obituaries and taking calls from angry readers. The copy desk ran a political cartoon in this morning's paper mocking the gun control stance of the Congressional senator from Winterborn, and the subscribers did not respond kindly. It's fine to mock a politician, even encouraged, it's fine to even mock a conservative politician, but it isn't fine to mock the only politician, conservative or not, to come out of our fair town. Even if people do say under their breath that he's an idiot, he's one of ours. Our idiot. The editorial staff fielded more than a few calls from readers threatening to cancel subscriptions and wanting to talk to Charles. I'm still new to the job, too thin skinned to not take their emotional reactions personally. Every complaint rattled me a bit.

But now Lucy's car is in the yard. I find her out on the deck drinking a beer and shooting a BB gun at sparrows. I'm already putting the day behind me.

"These little suckers are fast," she says, getting up to give me a hug. "How was your day?"

"Interesting. Meth arrests. City council dysfunction. A house fire that was the result of abject stupidity. Angry phone calls from readers all day. A pretty good news day for rural Nebraska."

"A pretty good news day for rural Nebraska," she says, smirking at me then firing another BB into the tree.

"My mom always said we couldn't kill the robins. The pigeons, yes. And you won't hit the sparrows. Shoot at them all you want. Hey, do you want to go to the hardware store? I need to pick up a couple of things."

She finishes her beer and I drive us to the store on the edge of town. All the sale items are placed by the front doors — garden tools, racks of seed packets, electric rototillers and the year's new lawnmowers. I'm in the back studying the deck paint when the clerk comes over, a scraggly beard and stains from his lunch break on his uniform polo.

"That stuff works like liquid cement," he says. "Best product they ever made. Put it on your deck and it'll last damn near forever."

"That's what we want," I say.

"Pick out a color and I'll mix it up while you check out the rest of the store."

We settle on a light oak and go over to the rows of pre-built bathroom cabinets.

"I could make one of these for a third of the cost," I say.

We pick out a sink, the wood and hardware for a cabinet, and I have the clerk mix up a few more buckets of paint for the walls. We load everything onto the truck. On the way back to the house Lucy says "You're really trying to make it work here, aren't you?"

"I figure if I'm going to be here."

"I don't see how you can do it."

"Might as well try."

"Better you than me."

I wake up thinking about the conversation with Falconer in Prime Cut and the increasing volume of letters to the editor, both for and against the Sun-Gazette's recent reporting. I go into the kitchen to make coffee with a sense of dread over the office phone ringing and the people who might show up at the open newsroom.

I eat breakfast then grab my tie, another part of the job I reject, but everyone knows Sue, the human resources manager, isn't going to forgo the outdated dress code as long as she still works there. She wants the office to remind her of the good ole days of the 1950s, back when she thought America was great. I knot my thrift store tie in a half Windsor, put on my blazer and step outside to get in my truck.

That's when I notice on the door of the white barn, in letters five feet high, the words LEAVE LIBERAL! in crude, red spray paint. I take out my phone and make a video, narrating "so this is what I woke up to this morning. I don't see any tracks. They must have parked on the road and walked into the yard."

I text the video to Lucy.

She replies: *You should take their advice.*

I go into the office feeling more sure of my purpose than before. I must be getting someone's attention to cause them to take that kind of action. I take the video to Guy.

He plays it and gets a big grin on his face.

"Congratulations," he says. "Looks like you have the topic for your first column. Tell the redneck idiots out there this isn't going to scare you. Don't call them rednecks, of course. Give me eight hundred words by lunch time. We'll run it tomorrow. Describe what happened. And explain how we're better than this as a community. Two more things then you can go get writing. Did you file a police report?"

"No."

"You probably should in case this turns into something bigger."

"Will do."

"The second thing is can I show this to Charles? I don't want him to be surprised by anything we print."

It's the easiest thing I have written to that point. I sit down, put my byline at the top of the page and it all comes out in a steady progression, word after word, line on line, until I have a personal column explaining what happened, what I imagine is the cause, my opinion of the cowards who did it, my vow not to be intimidated, and a couple of paragraphs publicly shaming their narrowmindedness and inability to debate in a civilized manner. I turn it in and Guy gives it a read before calling me into his office.

"This is a good start," he says. "But let me give you one piece of advice: You don't want to look like you're beating someone over the head in print. We have to try to be fair. As much as you don't want to — I mean, if it was me tonight I'd be sitting in my house with my lights off and a shotgun in my lap — you need to come off cool and unaffected by this. You don't want people to think you're easily rattled or they'll come after you even more. So I'm going to cut a few grafs. If you think they're necessary or the piece doesn't read right without them let me know and we can discuss it."

I trust Guy's judgment and his years on the job. I read over the story again at my desk and have no arguments.

When the column comes out the next day it goes as viral as anything I have written so far. More than a thousand likes and a few hundred shares on the Sun-Gazette's Facebook page. Scores of retweets on Twitter. Readers emailing me apologizing on behalf of the community and commending me for my measured handling of the situation.

I truly feel for the first time the power I have to convey my experiences through words, how I can reach people and connect to them through writing.

But it's not all support. One person comments on the Sun-Gazette's Facebook page under my column: "That spray paint said what plenty of us were thinking." That comment receives more than 20 likes of its own.

I text Lucy: *My story blew up!*

She responds: *Did it? I haven't read it.*
Read it!

I send her the link, but she doesn't respond.

While the column's success encourages me as a writer, for the moment I have more attention than I want. Charles focuses on the negative comment that received two dozen likes and calls Guy and me into his office.

His walls are decorated with framed pictures of deer and elk hunts and he has a bronze replica of a .270 rifle above the window behind his desk.

"We need to rethink our strategy on how we're covering the wastewater story," he says. "As in, we need to slow down."

"I disagree," Guy responds. "We're doing exactly what we need to be doing. I would be fairly certain that we're going to win awards for our coverage."

"And he's going to cost us plenty of subscribers in the meantime. Subscribers we can't afford to lose."

"Since when was that editorial's concern?" Guy asks.

"Since we've been dropping subscribers, losing at least a hundred a year, for the past ten years."

"That's just because the old people are dying. Regardless, this is a conversation that shouldn't involve Ethan."

"Why not? He should know the impact his stories are having on his community and his paycheck."

"Just so I get this straight — you're trying to lean on both of us."

"Let me read to you some of what we've printed as letters to the editor in our paper. 'Ethan Thomas and the Sun-Gazette's reporting has been some of the most anti-business journalism I've ever read. It's blatantly anti-American.' 'Ethan Thomas sounds like he's from Boulder.' 'If Ethan Thomas was ever really from here we should all consider that whatever he learned in Winterborn has been erased by California or whatever city he came back from. There's such a thing as too much education.'"

"Just because we printed them doesn't make them right," Guy says.

"But they do show how people in this community think."

"Some people. Again, that doesn't make them right."

"OK. Well, I didn't want to bring this up. I wanted to see how this conversation went first. But seeing as you two don't seem to be thinking of this newspaper as a business, let me give you both a little news. Our two biggest advertisers, the hospital and Small Town Growers, are going to pull their advertising completely if we don't stop writing about 'liberal topics,' including the environment. Now, just let that sink in before you say anything."

"I don't need to let that sink in," Guy says. "If you're telling me that our advertisers are dictating our editorial coverage than you need to ask yourself if you're running a newspaper or a public relations company. Because I'm not in P.R., I'm a journalist."

"A journalist who needs to eat."

"Not this bad I don't."

"Look," I say. "We started this whole ball rolling on the fracking fight. We can't stop now."

"We're not pulling back," Guy says.

"I'm proposing a temporary moratorium on any fracking stories," Charles says.

"Moratorium means temporary," Guy says.

"No way," I say. "We haven't published anything incorrect or libelous or harmful to the paper. There's no reason we should stop covering this story."

"He's right. You're going to have to fire

me before I agree to let you dictate coverage," Guy says.

"What about you, Ethan?" Charles asks.

"I'm with Guy."

"All right. We all should get back to work, but you two really need to cool it."

Lucy shows up at my house on a four-wheeler with her cowboy hat tied around her neck, smiling, a cloud of dust settling in her wake. Today's country music.

"Can you play?" she asks.

Internally I bristle at that silly language, but I'm not doing anything else, so I run inside and change my jeans then jump on behind her. The engine and the wind make it too loud to talk as we cross the pastures and farm fields to the river. When we stop at the gate I push the post toward the fence to slide the wire ring off the top, lift the post off the bottom ring of wire, fold it back to let her pass through, then hook it all back together again. Her smile widens a little more.

"I should have known you'd know how to

do that," she says when I hop back on.

At the river she turns off the vehicle and we step quietly through the grass down to the bank. She holds one finger to her lips and points to the treetops, her green eyes shining with energy. I look into the water and see minnows shooting under the surface.

"There," she says.

Above us a blue heron glides up into a nest, the pterodactyl-looking bird slow and graceful. Then another flies by. And another. In time there are at least a dozen of these large birds overhead, speaking in a guttural, primal cackle.

Lucy sits under a tall bush and takes pictures with a 35 millimeter film camera. I pick up a stick to lean on. Tufts of cotton float in the air, tracking slowly overhead like satellites. The grass pungent, the river a soft murmur.

We hear the gobbling of turkeys in the distant underbrush. When we go to look for them they scurry farther down the riverbank. I'm standing behind her, noticing the soft hair on her neck when an insect crawls down from her head and into her shirt.

"Shit," I say. "Don't move. Tick."

"Where?"

"Just crawled under your collar."

She screams and immediately takes off her shirt, shaking her head and waving her arms. She's running in circles, wide-eyed, half screaming. I laugh and wrap her in a hug. "Stop moving," I say. I catch the tick on her shoulder blade, crush it between my fingers and toss it in the grass.

"You might want to check your pants, too," I say. "You definitely want to take your pants off."

"Fuck."

"Or I could check them for you?"

"No. Yes. No. Let's go."

She runs to the four-wheeler.

"I'll drive," I say. "It seems a shame to tell you to put your shirt back on, but you might want to."

She rides back to the house pressed tightly against my back, letting out an intermittent "fuck."

There's an inevitability to all of this. Each interaction another moment in time that draws us closer. It feels slightly reckless to continue to see each other. Neither of us know what we really want, and we're unsure if we would even like each other in another place. But we're here now and it's been pretty fun so far. So why not continue? At least that's how it feels to me.

The next morning, I pull into the parking lot of the YMCA. The first light of the day shades the sky in hues of pink and orange. I pick up my phone and post a sunrise picture on Facebook.

"Moody sky," one friend writes. "I bet it's a little different seeing this from a sober Tuesday morning rather than a Sunday morning coming down."

That comment receives a few likes of its own from people I know in other places.

The locker room carpet smells of mold and chlorine. I change into nylon shorts, a t-shirt and tennis shoes. I begin my workout at the cable machine. From the squat rack comes guttural breathing, heavy grunts, man screams. I recognize the guy wearing a camouflage-pattern tank-top and black sweatpants. Tattoos cover one arm from his shoulder to his wrist, a menagerie of symbols and characters, much of it Asian.

"You're getting after it, aren't you?" I say when we meet at the water cooler.

"I don't fuck around when I get in here."

He seems to recognize me, but he also seems to be skeptical about the interaction, as though he isn't sure if he should invest much into our conversation. I could be projecting, but it feels like he's unsure what I'm doing here. Like I'm just home for a visit. I'm trying to attach meaning to these interactions, and the only thing I can come up with is we're both from this place, we're still alive, and that's about all I know. I doubt we'll speak again.

When I'm done with my workout and walking out I look up at the flocks of geese over the river, the black Vs in the bright sky. I have the sense that I'm still trying to figure out what I'm doing.

At the office, I've just booted up my computer when my phone rings. Mary Winslow. Another earthquake. Bigger this time and a strong aftershock. Two historic buildings on Main Street with broken windows and cracked walls. I travel to Arikaree with camera and notebook, speak to the merchants downtown, write down quotes and take detailed photographs of the damage.

Back at the office I write up the story, including the context of all the previous earthquakes, when the public first became aware of the wastewater injections, hearing Guy's voice in my head to put the most important information and illuminating details at the top of the story, then weave the remaining backstory in.

I save it, then let Guy know it's in. "20 inches in the queue on today's earthquake. With photos."

"I'll take a look," he says. "And hey, don't worry about what anyone else says. I think you're doing a great job."

I leave the office that day feeling full, a sense of having done a good day's work. What I'm writing isn't poetry, but I'm going out into the world and coming back with a story that people will read, and that feels about as true of a day's work as I can hope for.

I don't belong back here yet, and I don't know if I ever really will again, but I'm starting to think that's not as important to me as it once was. My role is to find stories and tell them, no matter where I am, or whether or not I belong.

I check Facebook and there it is — four of my best friends from high school, back for a weekend, all tagged in a photo at the rail-roaders' favorite bar. Lined up and smiling. The caption says #wheresethan. I get in my truck and drive down.

The bar is noisy with the conversation of drunk people who can't hear themselves very well. I recognize a few community members. My friends are in the back playing darts and laughing. I stop at the bar for a beer, then I join them. They're in full reminiscence mode.

"Do you remember Haley?" Dave asks. "She was so fucking hot. Ridiculous. I used to jerk off like crazy to the idea of banging her. Like every day."

"She has five kids now," Hal says. "Five."

"The Thompson twins," Peter says. "I kissed one of them once. Had no idea what I was doing. Still think about that sometimes. If I get one chance at time-traveling I'm not going back to kill Hitler. I'm going back to hit that shit right."

"But you live here now," Hal says, and the group turns its attention to me. "You don't need to go back down Memory Lane. You drive it every day."

"That must fucking suck," Dave says.

"I couldn't do it," says Peter.

"Why would you want to?" Hal says and they laugh.

"Do you ever regret coming back?" Peter asks. "I only ask because I would feel like I sold out, maybe."

"Not really," I say. "I have a plan. I mean, who's the bigger sell-out? The person who pretends to be something they're not? I've had your life. I know what it's like. Your independence doesn't really cure your loneliness, does it."

"Maybe not. But being anonymous is a helluva lot more fun," Hal says, and the guys laugh again. "I bet the grocery store's a nightmare."

"I'm going to grab another beer," I say, and I head to the bar.

I'm waiting for the bartender to come over when I'm bumped in the shoulder by a man's chest. The bar's not that crowded for this type of jostling.

"Your boss isn't here to protect you today," Dale Falconer says when I turn to face him. He smells like he's wearing Crown Royal cologne.

"Why would I need him to protect me?" I say.

Dale grabs me by the shirt at my chest and swings me into the table beside us. I fall into it and land on a chair. I try to get up but he's got me pinned between the furniture. He punches me in the eye twice while I'm trying to get up, and before I can get to my feet he grabs me by my belt and hurls me into the booth along the wall. I hit my head against the exposed brick and feel my neck pop. I try to get out of the booth but he's there with a boot that lands flat against my face, heel to chin, and my head snaps back against the wall. I have a moment to look out and see my friends standing by the bar, just watching. Falconer says "If you write about this I'm going to find you and do it again." I try to get out and he kicks me in the face. Then I'm out.

When I wake up I realize that my high school buddies left me there on the bench. I don't know how long I've been out, but business has resumed at the bar. The guys from school aren't there and neither is Falconer. I stand up and go the bathroom. My brow is swelling over my left eye and my chin is darkening from the heel of the cowboy boot. I have whiplash, a knot on the back of my head and sore ribs, but little blood, no teeth loose and nothing broken.

I get home and call Lucy, tell her what happened. She comes over, takes a bag of frozen corn from the freezer, wraps it in a washcloth and holds it to my face.

"Why are you doing this?" she says. "Is it worth it to try and be a writer if this is what's going to happen to you?"

"This isn't helping."

"I don't see how it's worth it."

"Fuck that guy."

"Is that it? You got your ass kicked in front of the whole town. Your face is all fucked up. And for what? Because you like seeing your name in the paper? I thought this would at least help you wake up. Stop dreaming."

"Oh I'm awake."

"You know you could be anything else but this."

"No. I can't be anything else. Especially not now."

She presses the corn into my eye and I take it from her.

"You're going to have to handle it from here," she says. "If you can't see that this is going to be a long, hard life than I can't help you."

I experience a palpable sense of doom as I park at the newspaper office the next morning. I don't want to answer any questions about this. But I go straight into Guy's office and before I can say anything he knows..

"This is where you tell me I should see the other guy," he says.

"The other guy was Dale Falconer."

"I heard. Goddammit."

"Jumped me at the bar."

"Did you ever file that police report?"

"No, I never did."

"Did you file one this time?"

"Doubt I will. Everyone already knows what happened."

"That's your call. But what he did isn't right. And shouldn't happen."

"I'm fine. Fuck him."

"The sheriff's probably going to want to talk to you. But you're right. Best thing you can do is get back to work."

I keep my head down and my phone stays quiet until the 10 a.m. editorial meeting. The other reporters all get up from their desks and file into the conference room with notebooks or laptops in hand. When I join them Guy is already in his chair at the end of the long table, hands folded behind his head, staring at a picture of a buffalo on the wall. He looks tired.

"Let's get started," he says, sitting up.

He goes around the room, calling on each reporter to share what story they're working on that day. Guy suggests sources to call or how to take photos. Once he has the day's coverage planned he assigns a pair of stories for the Sunday paper — an annual beet growers' meeting at the Civic Center and the governor speaking out at the airport.

"But the main thing we need to talk about today is fracking wastewater injections," he says, his voice serious, tinged with disgust. "I'm sure you've heard about this. Well, I've been given a direct order from corporate to halt our wastewater coverage until further notice. As you know Ethan has been doing a great job with his reporting, even taken a few lumps for it, but the people who sign our checks believe we have shown some type of bias with the amount of our coverage and want us to write about other topics for a while. I don't believe we've done anything wrong, but it won't hurt us to lay off it for the time being. We all know there are tons of other stories out there, so this shouldn't be a problem."

I can't quite figure out how to react. I see Jerry looking at me.

"Right. Like there are bigger stories out

there than man-made earthquakes," Jerry says. "I'm going over to the library today to photograph the new bench they're installing. Some real hard-hitting journalism there. Maybe that should be a series. Ethan, are you going to let them do this to you? Are you going to let Charles and Dale Falconer take you off the biggest story to come around in years?"

I'm thinking about what I should say when Guy says "I wish he had a choice. This is a clear directive from management."

"You mean from the advertisers," Jerry says.

"Hey, I don't like this anymore than anyone else," Guy says. "Charles telling me how to run this paper is like me telling a nuclear power plant operator how to do the job. He has no idea what he's talking about. But this is where we are in today's newspaper world. If we lose our revenue sources we lose our jobs. I knew this day was coming for a long time. Now it's finally here, and it sucks. I always hoped I'd be retired before something put me in this position. I'm old, but I'm not that old yet."

Guy gets up from his chair, signaling that he doesn't want to discuss the matter further. I shuffle back to my desk feeling as though a major shift is occurring. I'm in a moment that, depending on how I react, could affect the course of my career for years.

"Are you going to let them do this to you? To us?" Jerry calls to me across the newsroom. "I wouldn't let them do this to me. I'd tell them where to shove it."

I sit down and text Lucy.

You won't believe what just happened.

Guy just pulled me off the wastewater story.

Said none of the reporters can write about fracking anymore.

> *Are you surprised?*

Not really, but it sucks.

> *Is this because of the bar fight?*

Guy says it's not.

> *You should quit.*

I don't want to give up that easy.

> *I don't see why you're so stubborn about this. Journalism is dead. You can find another career.*

Maybe. But I'm not walking away like this.

I come home to a freshly painted living room. Blue tape marks the edges of tan walls. Lucy has painted the wood of the door frames and the baseboards white. The stereo's up loud. I stand there watching her work, in her thrift store t-shirt and cutoff jean shorts. I kiss her on the back of the neck.

"Don't smell me," she says. "I've been working."

"I know. I like it."

I take two beers from the fridge and bring her one.

"This is every girl's fantasy right here," she says. "A guy who brings her beer while she's doing manual labor. Hey, why don't we go for a drive."

It's quiet. I watch the highway. On the far edge of the valley, past the rundown farmhouses and the closed brick country school and the pastureland with a few skinny bay horses, the iron gray clouds of a storm creep up over the cottonwood trees on the side of the lake.

"Even in summer, even when it's all green, this place looks empty," Lucy says. "How can the sky feel this heavy?"

I leave the radio off, the only sound the tires bumping over the tar highway connectors and bugs tapping against the windshield.

"When was the last time you were out here?"

"It's been a while."

"But you remember where to go, right?"

"Of course."

I drive around to the back of the lake where the pavement ends and follow the dirt road to the pulloff at the end. Through a grove of cottonwoods and onto the sand. I back up to the edge of the water, put the tailgate down and we sit watching the boats and jet skis. Fishermen in the coves. A lone seagull above.

"I need to tell you something," she says, in a quiet tone, looking out over the lake.

I don't say anything.

"You know that we both don't belong here."

"We don't?"

"We don't. At least I know I don't. You're not going to like this, but I'm moving to Montana," she says. "I have a friend who manages a hotel there and she can get me a job."

"Sounds about right," I say.

I kick at the soft sand where the lake laps at the beach.

"When were you going to tell me?" I ask.

"Now. I was going to tell you now."

The sky dims quickly. I watch the sun fail to stay up behind the trees. The day ends. We need jackets.

"There's a high school game tonight," I say. "Could you handle it?"

"Absolutely not," she says.

"We have to do something," I say. "Let's go to a movie."

She curls up her chin and pauses a moment before glancing up at me.

"OK."

We drive to the historical theater in Ari-karee. She doesn't speak in the car. The sky is lit up like an upside down phosphorescent ocean, pink and orange and deep blue. The clouds the coral. The jet streams neon white tails of sharks. I turn the radio up.

We park on the old main street with most of the businesses boarded up. Aside from the theater, only two bars and the American Legion have lights on.

The previews have started. She doesn't grab my hand, but she doesn't move it when I place it on her leg.

"I hate you," I think but don't say.

The lights dim. The lion roars. She shifts in her seat and makes jokes during the movie. "This is terrible," she whispers. "Look at them. I can practically see the holes in their faces from the Botox injections. Can you imagine what they smell like?"

We get up as soon as the credits roll. Walk out silent. But when we get in the car I snort and look out the window.

"Such a fucking cliché," I say. "You saw on TV somewhere that all cowgirls need to live in the American West."

"No. That's not it. I just want to see some of the world before I get too old," she says.

"You got tricked by the Travel channel. You read too many National Geographics."

"I want to get the fuck out of Nebraska. This is just—"

"—something you have to do. I know. You've said that before."

"I should stay here and work for my parents forever and be miserable?"

"You could do anything you want."

"And what should that be?"

"Anything. That's what you always tell me. I know one thing you could do. You could stay."

"And be miserable."

"I'm glad I make you miserable."

"It isn't about you. It's about leaving here."

"And leaving me."

"Look. I'll call you. I'll write to you. We have technology. We can make it work. When you're ready to stop screwing around and playing writer you can come to Montana."

"It's amazing how you still don't get me. You think I'm just playing at this."

"You need to get out of here, too. Figure out what you really want."

"Is that what you're going to do in Montana? Figure out what you really want?"

"I just want to have some experiences."

"You just want to have some experiences," I say. "Maybe I do, too. That ever cross your mind? Maybe that's what I'm going to do, too. Have some experiences."

We're close to her house.

"Don't take me home yet," she says.

I pull over and get out. We stand in the center of the dirt road, looking up at the night sky. It looks like how you would paint the stars if you wanted to exaggerate how many you can see.

Until I start listening there is no sound. Then I detect layers of noise. The wind rustles the cottonwoods on the edge of the pasture. Crickets rub their legs together, chirping on a frequency almost too high to place. Cars pass down on the highway in a fleeting, low swoosh. I wait for the train's horn, drag my foot across the road to alter the sonic composition.

"I'm leaving next week," she says.

Then I can hear the train.

"Good," I say.

"Good? Is that all you have to say?"

"I think that's the right move for you. You can go have some experiences."

She laughs.

"Take me home," she says. "I'm tired."

Lucy walks in my house without knocking and into my bedroom. She stands before me smiling in a white dress, then takes off the straps and unzips the back. Nothing underneath. She steps toward me. I pop open the pearl snaps on my shirt and she laughs.

She smells like she's just showered and put on deodorant. Her skin soft, warm. I lean down to kiss her. We go to the bed together and lay down on our sides, both of us smiling, aware of our breathing. In a lithe movement she's on top of me. She knows what she's doing — long, slow strokes that build into quick, violent thrusts, then back down to slow again. She narrows her eyes. Leans back. She slides a hand down my stomach to touch herself, making quick circles with her fingers.

She slows down to steady, deep moves. I dig my fingers into her thighs.

After it ends we're still here. The air re-enters the room and I'm back in my body again. I dress and go downstairs. She meets me out on the porch. She has on her best denim jacket over her dress, a crumpled up straw hat and worn leather boots.

We sit on the deck chairs and Lucy rolls a cigarette. Dew sparkles on the tips of the grass in the lawn. Blackbirds sing in the hackberry tree. She lets her dog out of the back of the truck to run and the Lab sprints for the trees, sniffing at the bases of the cottonwoods.

She hands me a tupperware container, a handmade card and a notebook and pens..

"Happy birthday," she says. "You can get some writing done now that I'm leaving and you're not spending all your free time with me. Do you like hummus?"

She opens it up, lifts a glob with her finger and feeds it to me.

"Tastes a little like dirt," I say.

"I thought you'd been somewhere."

"Apparently not."

I listen for the train but can't hear it, the sound of her still echoing in my ears.

"You're going to call me, right?" she asks.

"Sure."

The dog comes over. I find the spot behind his ear he likes.

"OK. Time to get going. Enjoy Nebraska. I'll send you something from the road."

She loads the dog up and drives slow out of the yard, waving over the steering wheel as she heads north on the highway.

"That's why this place doesn't work," Carrick is telling me that night in between sips of gin and tonic. His face is gray, long. His eyes blend with the shadows from the dim bar lights. When he talks it's like he doesn't care if he's there or not. "We have all the land we could imagine all around us. But it's not yours. It's not mine. It's all owned. It's all a reminder of the money other people have. Winterborn and the county are pieces owned by other people. Your family used to own plenty of land around here. You know what it's like to live in the country. That's a great life."

"It's still pretty easy here in town," I say, leaning back into the booth.

"Exactly," he says, pointing at me. "That's exactly what it is. Easy. It's mind-numbing. Brutally fucking mind-numbing."

"So leave. That seems to be in style."

"I have. Those other places are less mine than this one."

"You can make them yours," I say in a tone that I immediately think is too dismissive. "Other people do it every day."

"No one does. Those places that are full of people from other places? They're still owned by someone. Usually by the people who stayed."

"You sound like you made up your mind. Winterborn sucks. And so does everywhere else."

He shrugs. "I need to either live out in deep country, wilderness, or I need to be in a real city. I can't do this halfway small town shit."

I consider that there are likely several people in the bar listening to us talk. "Then move out to the country. Why are you still complaining?"

"I need someone to do it with me. I can't be alone like that. When I lost Maribel I lost everything." He looks down at his hands.

"People always say that time will fix things," I say. "But we both know that's not true. I mean, gradually you start to fill up your life with other people and you'll think more about them than you do her. But that's no guarantee that you won't be blindsided by memories. We don't get over other people."

"That's definitely not helping."

"Shut up and get us another beer."

"Wait. I'm not done with this." He spreads his hands in the gesture of a question. "What if all this moving around, all these relationships, fucking college, all of it, what if we've just made our adult lives worse? We're always told to go get experiences, to date a lot of people, see a lot of things, so we'll know what we want. But maybe that's terrible advice. I still want to be with most of the girls I dated. I mean, there were some awful relationships in there, but so many of them fell apart for random reasons. I always thought there'd be another experience, and that having more experiences meant I was living a full life, when maybe all I was really doing was making it harder to love the next person. Maybe our parents were right. Maybe marrying your high school sweetheart is the best possible way. And staying where you're from. The place you know. Every beautiful place I've moved away from is someone I loved once that I can't be with anymore."

I nod my head. "You can't go back to places. They're never the same."

"I've revisited places I loved, and either they'd changed or I was different. The same for relationships. At what point do we stop having new experiences and start trying to repeat the ones that we can't have again or failed at the first time?"

"I definitely don't have the answer to that."

Carrick looks around at the bar and the people in it. "God I hate this place," he says. "This fucking town."

"You know. One thing I've learned," I say. "Is that there's nothing more unattractive than someone who's ashamed of where they're from."

"You're not going to convince me that

this town isn't a shithole," Carrick says, shaking his head. "I don't care if that's ugly. It's the truth."

He gets up for another round. When he comes back I change the subject.

Guy orders pizza and has us gather in the conference room. He's back from the state press association awards where the Sun-Gazette won the sweepstakes award for daily newspapers in our circulation category. We won first place in breaking news, breaking news photography and in-depth reporting, among other awards.

"This is the first I know of that we've won this many awards," Guy says, standing in front of the pizza boxes. "Thanks to the frackers. We did a lot of great work this year, despite plenty of resistance to our efforts. But this sweepstakes award validates everything we were doing. You all should be proud."

The day plays out and I stay until all the 8-5 workers go home. When the newsroom empties out save for copy editors and the sports desk, I gather my stuff and walk out to my truck. This has gone a lot differently than I thought it would. I've learned plenty, both about writing and the place where I was raised. I'm completely uncertain of the future, but I know one thing — I'm a writer now. I don't know yet how good of one, but I'm not worried about that. I've found something to dedicate my life to.

Back home I open the door to a still house. I'm no longer hopeful that Lucy might be there, waiting with a surprise. I think back on her: sitting on the porch with a BB gun; standing on a ladder painting a wall; coming out of the shower in a red and white gingham dress. I want to text her that I miss her but I don't. I just walk outside and look out over the valley, the only noise the silence, then the sounds reveal themselves, one by one.

Thank you to Adam Gnade, Rich Baiocco, Mark Galaritta, and Benjamin Whitmer for reading this in draft form and helping to make it better. Also, big thanks to Nate Perkins for putting it out into the world.

Bart Schaneman lives in Denver, Colorado, where he works as a business reporter covering the cannabis industry. He was raised on a farm in Nebraska, has worked as a journalist for 15 years, and lived in Asia for five. He is the author of the novel *The Green and the Gold*, the travelogue *Trans-Siberian* and the collection of essays *Someplace Else: On Wanderlust, Expatriate Life, & the Call of the Wild*.

Cactus
by Nathaniel Kennon Perkins

In *Cactus*, correctional officer and ex-punk rocker Will Stephens works guarding prisoners who pick up trash on the side of the highway. One of them, a hardened inmate with a tattoo of the Black Flag logo right beneath his eye, seems oddly familiar, but Will can't quite place him.

Sixty Tattoos I Secretly Gave Myself at Work
by Tanner Ballengee

STISGMAW is the most beautiful, the most vulnerable of punk and adventure memoirs. Each vignette centers around a hand-poked tattoo that the author gave himself while on the clock.

The Pocket Peter Kropotkin
Collected in this cute, pocket-sized volume are eight of Kropotkin's essays. The book starts with his indispensable article on anarchism, originally written for the Eleventh Edition of the *Encyclopedia Britannica*, and moves forward to expound on his ideas, which include prison abolition, syndicalism, expropriation, etc.

Order at tridentcafe.com